For Georgie and Harry – L.G.
Emmie and Sophie – H.P.

Farshore

First published in Great Britain 2021 by Farshore

An imprint of HarperCollins*Publishers*
1 London Bridge Street, London SE1 9GF
www.farshore.co.uk

HarperCollins*Publishers*
1st Floor, Watermarque Building, Ringsend Road
Dublin 4, Ireland

Text copyright © Louise Greig 2021
Illustrations copyright © Hannah Peck 2021
Louise Greig and Hannah Peck have asserted their moral rights.

The illustrated character of Ed is based on an original character
illustrated by Júlia Sardà in the title *Sweep* by Louise Greig.

ISBN 978 1 4052 9939 8
Printed in China.
001

A CIP catalogue record for this title is available from the British Library.

Green

Louise Greig

Hannah Peck

Farshore

Green was gone.
Winter had turned Green to White.

White meant one thing to Ed.
White meant . . .

Sled!

And Ed's sled meant
that Ed was the happiest.

His smile was
the biggest.

His sled gleamed.
His sled was fast.
It would stop his friends
in their tracks.

Ed froze.

Purple, orange, yellow and red flashed past.
New and shiny. Sleek and fast.

Suddenly Ed's sled seemed
old and dull and slow.
His smile slid into the snow.

Ed trudged back to his shed.
He set to work to build a **spectacular** sled.
A sled that would freeze everyone in their tracks.

Through bitter days and nights Ed stayed in his shed.

Just when he thought his sled might be ready,
a frosty voice inside his head said,
Not quite.

BEST SLED

• BIG
• SPACE FOR HATS
• TELESCOPE

Not quite the biggest.
Or the fastest.
Or the best.

Yet.

Through ice
and sleet and wind
he toiled on.

Ed turned numb.
He longed to come out of his shed.
He knew he was missing out
on all the fun in the snow.
But the icy voice inside him said,
No. Ed. Not. Yet.

Ed's friends missed him. They called, *Ed!*
But Ed did not hear them.
He did not see them.
He saw only his sled.

The days grew longer.
The sun shone stronger.
The air wafted . . .

warmer?

At last Ed's spectacular sled was ready to go.

He set off up the steep hill.

He did not see blue peeping out of the snow.

He did not hear the blackbird's lilting song.

But he did feel a . . . *PLIP!*

And another.

And another.

Plip-plip-plip. Plop.

Stop! Ed gulped.

But the rain ignored him.

It poured down on White.

And with each huge drop

Ed watched White turn to . . .

Ed sat slumped by his sled.

The slopes shimmered white with daisies.

My sled was the best, he sighed.

It was the biggest.

It was . . .

Just then a *tring* rang in Ed's ears.
He heard his friends shout,

Ed!

Purple, orange, yellow and red sparkled in the sun!

The wheels began to turn . . .

The warmth of spring seeped in.
It melted Ed's heart.
His smile lit up the valley below.

It stopped his friends in their tracks.
Where have you been, Ed?
We have missed you!

Ed looked at his sled;
I have been in my shed.

He felt a bit silly.

Now wheels whizzed together in the wind
and Ed's head spun with happiness.

His smile was the biggest.
His laughter was the loudest.
Ed is the best! sang his friends.

Green spilled through the grass
and the trees all spring and all summer long.

All the snow was gone.

When Ed thought about his sled he laughed.
And when he heard the rumble of wheels in the valley
and felt a whirl of joy in his heart he knew,
anything can turn around!